Mousekin's Special Day

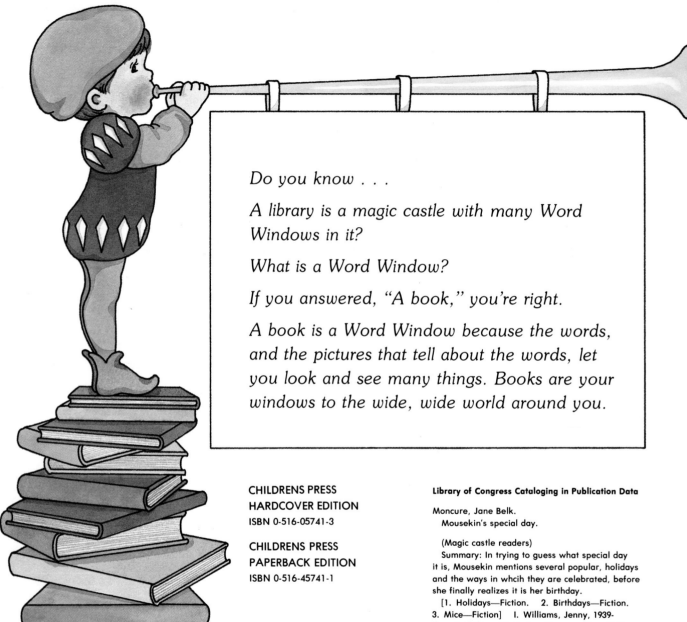

Do you know . . .

A library is a magic castle with many Word Windows in it?

What is a Word Window?

If you answered, "A book," you're right.

A book is a Word Window because the words, and the pictures that tell about the words, let you look and see many things. Books are your windows to the wide, wide world around you.

CHILDRENS PRESS
HARDCOVER EDITION
ISBN 0-516-05741-3

CHILDRENS PRESS
PAPERBACK EDITION
ISBN 0-516-45741-1

Library of Congress Cataloging in Publication Data

Moncure, Jane Belk.
  Mousekin's special day.

  (Magic castle readers)
  Summary: In trying to guess what special day it is, Mousekin mentions several popular, holidays and the ways in whcih they are celebrated, before she finally realizes it is her birthday.
  [1. Holidays—Fiction.   2. Birthdays—Fiction. 3. Mice—Fiction]   I. Williams, Jenny, 1939- ill.   II. Title.   III. Series: Moncure, Jane Belk. Magic castle readers.
PZ7.M739Mo 1988   [E]   87-11750
ISBN 0-89565-366-4

Mousekin's Special Day

by Jane Belk Moncure
illustrated by Jenny Williams

Created by
THE CHILD'S WORLD

Distributed by CHILDRENS PRESS®
Chicago, Illinois

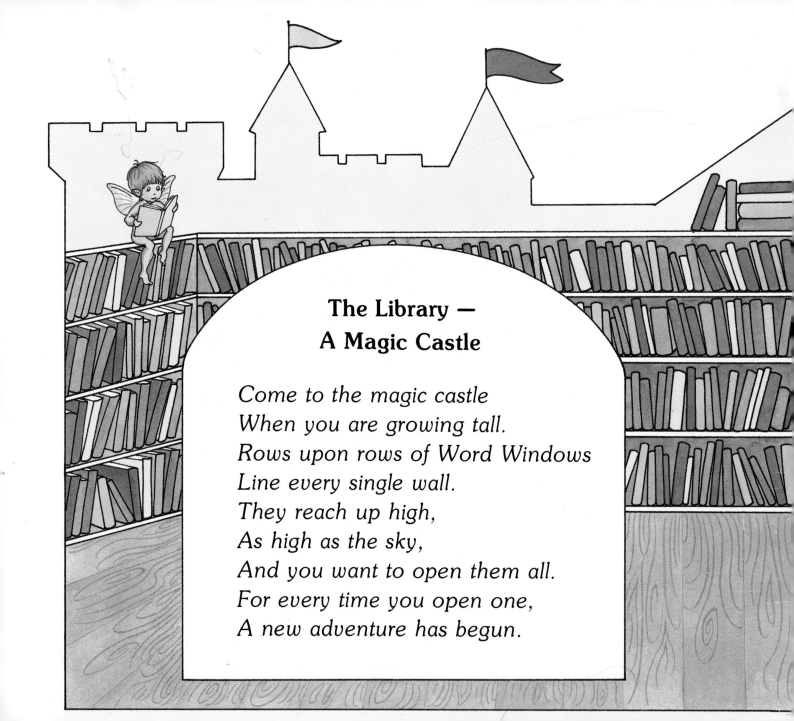

The Library —
A Magic Castle

Come to the magic castle
When you are growing tall.
Rows upon rows of Word Windows
Line every single wall.
They reach up high,
As high as the sky,
And you want to open them all.
For every time you open one,
A new adventure has begun.

Jenny opened a Word Window
in the magic castle. Here is
what she read.

"Wake up, Mousekin," said Mama
Mouse. "This is your special day."

"What special day?" asked Mousekin.
"You know," said Mama Mouse.

"Is today Valentine's Day?" asked Mousekin, smiling.

"No," said Mama Mouse. "This is not Valentine's Day. We have no valentines in this mouse house today."

"Is today Easter Day?" asked Mousekin.

"No, this is not Easter
Day," said Mama.
"We have no Easter basket
in this mouse house today."

"Maybe this is the Fourth of July,"
said Mousekin, as she played her
drum . . . tum, tum, tum.

"No," said Mama Mouse. "You know this is not the Fourth of July. We have no flags in this house today."

"What are you making?" asked Mousekin.

"A surprise," said Mama Mouse.
"Now run outside and play."

Mousekin played with her ball. "This ball looks like a pumpkin. It makes me think of another special day."

She ran into the house. "Is
today Halloween?" she asked.

"No," said Mama Mouse. "You know this is not Halloween.

"We have no jack-o-lanterns in this mouse house today."

"Well," said Mousekin. "If this is not Valentine's Day, or Easter, or the Fourth of July,

or Halloween, maybe it is . . .

Thanksgiving Day today. Maybe we
will have a Thanksgiving party."

"We will have a party, but not a Thanksgiving party," said Mama Mouse. "Guess again."

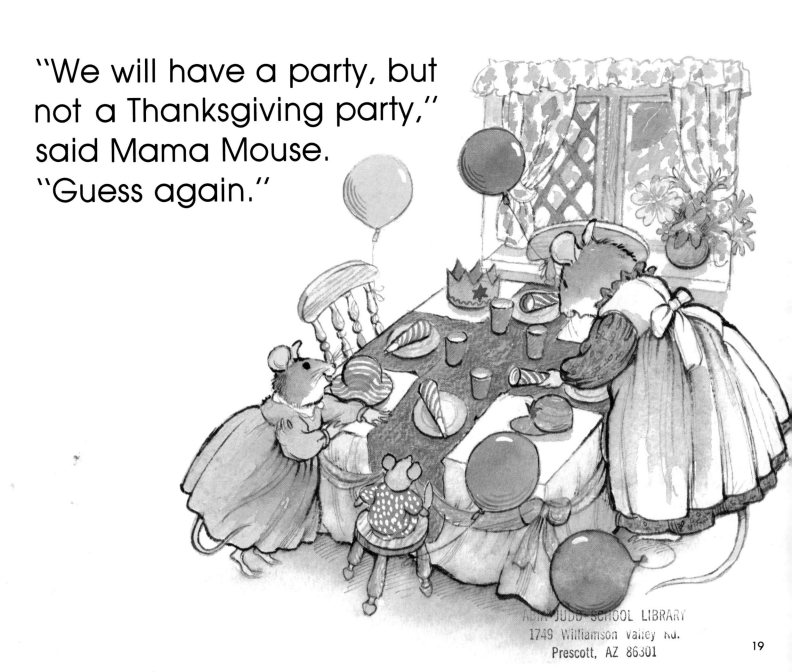

"I cannot think of another
special day," said Mousekin.

"Yes, you can," said Mama Mouse.

Just then, Papa Mouse came into the house with a gift.

"Hurrah," said Mousekin. "This must be Christmas."

"No," said Papa Mouse. "You know it is not Christmas." Then Mama Mouse put a big cake on the table.

"Now I know," said Mousekin, jumping up and down. "Today is someone's birthday."

"Yes," said Mama Mouse. "It is the birthday of someone very special."

"Is it your birthday, Mama?"
Mama shook her head no.

"Is it your birthday, Papa?"
Papa shook his head no.

"Then it must be my birthday,"
said Mousekin. "This is my own
special day. I knew it all along."

"Happy Birthday, Mousekin," said her friends.

"A happy birthday is the very best special day of all," Mousekin said.

Jenny closed the Word Window.

You can read these special-day words.

Valentine's Day

St. Patrick's Day

Easter

Fourth of July

Happy Birthday

Halloween

Thanksgiving Day

Christmas

Here are some more special days around the year.

May Day

Mother's Day

Hanukkah

Father's Day

Can you name more?